FIRST ROUND DRAFT PICK

Will "Rico" Davis

authorHOUSE®

AuthorHouse™
1663 Liberty Drive
Bloomington, IN 47403
www.authorhouse.com
Phone: 833-262-8899

Published by AuthorHouse 07/30/2021

ISBN: 978-1-6655-3209-9 (sc)
ISBN: 978-1-6655-3216-7 (e)

Print information available on the last page.

The Introduction

Who will be the next first round draft pick? Will she be a free agent or just on the practice squad?

Take this journey with Davante as he explores with 4 beautiful women from 4 different cultural backgrounds. He must choose a soulmate that he emotionally, physically and spiritually connects with. Someone not only would he consider his best friend, but someone he can put all his trust and heart into regardless of nationality.

Chapter 1

IT'S A BEAUTIFUL Monday morning and Davante does his normal routine starting at 8am, he gets up make himself some breakfast and check his emails while watching sports center. He is living the bachelors life. Whenever his kids are not spending a night at his home it's normally so quiet you could hear a pin drop. He does miss his two kids on a regular being around the house and waking up with the same women every morning.

Davante gets on the phone and called up John and Greg the two of his best friends that are still married. He was able to get in contact with John 1st. Hey what's going on dude? Hey what's up Davante, you know, the same old shit just another day. "I here you". "I'm in town this week, so are we hitting the gym today"? If so, you already know it's Monday and that's chest, triceps and abs day. John said you know I'm good, but 1st I have to drop my wife off at her moms house because her car is in the shop. So I will meet you guys up there about 5:30pm. Ok cool, that's good because Greg's wife is dropping him off at the gym around that time while she shop at the mall across the street. See you guys later. As Davante drives to the gym, he stopped by the smoothie shop to get his favorite protein shake as a meal replacement. Hey Davante how are you today. I'm good Jerry. Do you want your same old. Yes I do. From the looks of this weather it seems like we might be getting some rain today Jerry. I heard the weather man mentioned it today, but honestly Devante the weather man has been given false weather report for quite sometime. So at this point if it rains it rains if it doesn't it doesn't. "Laugh out loud" I hear that. Ok sir that's going to be $7.99 plus tax. Ok you can put it on this card right here. Ok thank you sir. Have a great day Jerry. You too Davante.

As Davante leaves the shop he pushes the button on his keychain to start up his black on black Lamborghini. Two teenagers that were walking towards Davante as he was approaching his vehicle said wow dude that is a phat ride. Man I can only dream to have a car like that.

Davante said you don't have to dream. All you need is 3 things and you can drive one just like this or better. You need a vision and a plan and then you execute. Dude thanks for that advice. No problem kid.

Sir are you a professional athlete or a salesman. Davante said neither. I'm a Sports Agent. You guys have a good day. You too sir. Thank you.

Now as Davante pulls up to the gym It's now closer to 5pm it's hard finding a good parking spot, so he continues driving through the parking lot until he get lucky to see someone leaving the gym. After two circle around the parking lot. Today must be a good day because Davante saw and older lady leaving and she was parked right up front. He ask the lady please tell me your leaving. She jokingly said no I'm just putting something in my car. He was like nooooooo.

Then she was like I'm just kidding, it's all yours. Davante was like thank you ma'am.

So as Davante walked into the gym he decided to sit in the Cyber cafe to kill time because like always he will be at the gym before John and Greg because they are never on time. So as he sit in the lobby watching sports center. He notice Lori sitting down watching sports center as well. She is the girl that every time we come here to the gym she's at the gym either leaving or coming. But this time would be different because for the 1st time they will actually have an opportunity to have a full conversation besides saying hello or bye. So he walked up to Lori and ask if this seat was taken. She was like hey stranger, no it's not. He was like cool. Well I just need a seat until my two late friends John and Greg shows up. It looks like you really watching that Sports Center. Well that's because I really am watching it. Ohhhhhh fisty.

He ask Lori are you a big football fan?

Lori responded by saying how do you know? Well two things your keychain on the counter has the Houston Texas symbol and that Sports Center that you so focused on seem to really have your attention. Wow Davante you are very observant I'm impressed. Let's just say I pay attention to details.

Lori responded with well I have to represent my hometown and actually, I fell asleep last night on the Monday night football game, so I was trying to see how many running yardage did Adrian Foster finish with since the team record is at 500 now and in 2nd place of the AFC.

Davante was certainly impressed and blown away by Lori's beauty and the fact that she knows her football. In a million years I would have never known that Lori would get that deep into a profession I make my living from. Ok I think I need to take a seat. Do you mind? No help your self. They sat down and talked about a lot of things. She couldn't believe that I was single and likewise I told her that it's hard to believe that she is single as well. He explained that due to him traveling and negotiating Professional contracts, like one day he's here in Florida, the next day he's in Seattle. A lot of the ladies he have met throughout the years, when he explained that it has been hard for him to settle down especially after college football season, his profession requires a lot of traveling and recruiting. It would take an understanding women to except his line of work. He cater to athletes, because they provide his lifestyle. Ok enough of me and my occupation, tell me some things about Ms Lori, besides her knowing her football. Well the short version, I'm from Houston. I have been here in Florida for about 3 years. Single, no kids, love working out and eating healthy. I have my own marketing firm. So I guess I'm just like you. My focus is my career. I have my moments, but I would need a man who can add to what I have and hopefully he understands my profession as well. If he does he will find himself a damn good women. Oh really, yes really. Ok I'm not mad at you. What's that your drinking? Oh this is my favorite protein shake call the Gladiator. It's a post workout shake with natural fiber, bananas, peanut butter, and protein. Wow that sounds delicious. I'm definitely going to try that one day.

I normally drink it after my workouts. See I'm already on my post drink, while you and your friends are just getting started. I had my pre shake just before you walked in. I try to get here earlier to the gym, but I have these calls I have to make and besides I normally workout with my two friends. So it's like what's best for everyone. Well if you come a lil earlier in the day, maybe we can workout together. But that's only if you can keep up. Ohh you have jokes.

Ok here comes my two homeboys. Now promise me we will definitely finish our conversation another time? I promise you, we will. Ok cool, well It was nice chatting with you, I'm sure I will see you around in the gym again. Ok sounds good, now just to give you heads up, I probably won't be here closer to the holidays since my family lives in Houston, Texas. I normally fly home for Christmas every year, but I'm hoping they will start flying here after this year. So three weeks of no gym and lots of food and my family driving me crazy. We gotta love our family. Trust me I know the feeling. I thought it was just my family that was crazy. Ok I'm sure I will see you again take care. You too.

What's good man, you guys ready to put this workout in. Yes indeed. Man I see you talking to my girlfriend Lori. That's your girl. She will be if I get a divorce. Lori is fine and she works out. Man you are silly. No she gets to the gym before you two late birds. So we just chat every time we get a moment. She is real cool and down to earth. Man what is her nationality, I believe her mother is Black and her father is white. She mention something like that to me one day I saw her at the gym. Ok let's get down on these weights. I'm going 1st, who gonna spot me.

I got you. Oh yeah before I forget, how was that lil spot where you guys for happy hour.

Man I be wanting to go, but my wife is not hearing that. She'll be like you better have your happy hour ass drinks in the house. Man you crazy. I tell my wife the same thing. She thinks if we go we just looking at women. Hell I tell her I'm not looking at men. Man I got 15 years in this marriage, she know I'm not going nowhere but in the next room if she gets on my nerves. I can honestly say man I have a good marriage. I'm not gonna mess that up. Davante that's what you need in your life. A good woman who's got your back. You need a ride or die chick. Man it's funny you said that because that's what I'm dealing with right now dude. I'm so ready to take a chance at love. I believe love is blind. So I'm willing to love whoever my heart excepts.

So to make a long story short fellas

I'm thinking about settling down. Greg was like, settling down from what? Working out?

I'm like, I see you got jokes. John was like you sure you ready man. You know once you make that commitment a lot of the freedom and flexibility you had will come to a stop. I told the guys I know man, but I have been really doing lots of thinking and soul searching. This dating game is cool. But it's been two years since my divorce.

When females meet me they already assume I'm in a relationship, they assume I'm happily married and when they find out I'm single. They are very much surprised or they ask the question is something wrong with you. It may look like I have everything together on the outside, but to be honest, I feel lonely because I don't have a true soulmate. Me being single have been my choice and it gave me time to focus on a lot things that I needed to work on as a person. And I couldn't expect to make another person happy until I find happiness within myself 1st.

It's kinda like you two. You both are married to your soulmate and I'm sure you are in love and I'm sure you feel complete. See that's what I'm missing. And lately, I have been really thinking about marriage once again. Being a sports agent allows me the flexibility to move anywhere, but I would prefer to stay here in Florida because of my kids. My ideal women would be the type that could walk in a room and everything stops. I picture her as someone that is sexy, her looks would make the average man afraid to approach her. But her personality would be sweet as a dove. I would like for her to be a people's person, outgoing, not shy and all about her business. But lately every woman I have met its more like a relationship test. I'm only looking for marriage material women. I'm not going to waste anymore time with a woman I have no plans to marry. That way I can finally get to the point where I can introduce them to my kids.

Now I must say there have been four beautiful ladies who fit all these descriptions.

I was just keeping them in the friend zone. Because I knew once I cross that line with either one of them it could ruin that friendship if it's really not meant to be. One of my biggest fears, is we both invest time with each other and it doesn't work out. Would it be enough to call it quits or hang in there and work it out. I'm not gonna lie, I got on my knees and prayed that whatever decision I make I hope is the right one. But at this point guys, I wanna call that one woman, my only woman. Greg was like so what are you planning on doing with the other friends you have? I told him, that's just it. I have met some amazing women and each one has something special about them. But it's not just that. Not only am I about to settle down, my option is now open for any women of any race. John was like man are you sure you want to step that far out. You never dated outside your race. I know that's it. I've never, so I don't want to miss out on my soulmate because I only dated my race. This is an adjustment that I'm willing to except.

I have four amazing women that I'm really cool with. I have a lot of traveling coming up, so I will make effort to spend quality time with each one of them. I feel after this I will be able to know if there is really chemistry outside my race and if these women are different because of there nationally. Greg, Wow Davante is looking for true love. Man I'm not mad at you. Like you said me and John already found our soulmate. I know man, I want that also. I thought I had that with my ex-wife. But really, it wasn't what I truly wanted. But God blessed us with two amazing kids. It's seems we were better off just being friends.

Ok guy's enough of me. Let's get this workout in because I got some business calls to make this afternoon.

Chapter 2

Hispanic

IT'S MONDAY AFTERNOON, and he's on the phone with a potential clients father whom he happens to be good friends with, called Davante and said that his sons team won last night in the Elite 8 NCAA basketball tournament. So at that moment he knew it was time for him to head down to Atlanta.

He asked the dad how did he play. He said that his son had a career high with a triple double.

Davante was like that's what I love to hear. The dad said "Davante ever since you gave my son that one on one talk his game has elevated to the next level". Davante explained that the fire has always been inside your sons game we just needed someone different from his parents to help him light that fire. Right now with the mock draft they projecting your son a lottery pick maybe going between the 8th and 10th. With stats like this, if he keeps this up he will definitely climb that draft board and become one of the top 3 picks.

So Davante called up one of his homeboys and said not sure what you got going on this weekend, but lets take this trip to Atlanta for the NCAA final four. I must be at this game, because my future client is my prize possession and one of the high profile players In this years tournament. He knew he had a good opportunity of representing his son after he declares for the NBA draft. John said I'm good for this weekend, just let me know what time you wanna take off and I'm good. I'm thinking Friday morning. That's cool with me. So they jump in the truck Friday morning and took that five hour drive from Jacksonville, Florida to Atlanta, Georgia.

Once they got on the outskirts of Atlanta, traffic was crazy. When they finally made it to Atlanta their first stop was the Lenox mall. The mall was so packed even VIP parking was crazy.

They had to wait almost 30 minutes for Valet to take the keys. Once they finally made it inside the mall they saw fans representing there school pride. They ran into a lot of former NCAA players who are currently playing in the NBA and some that play professionally overseas.

It seems Atlanta was definitely the place to be this weekend and we were just getting our day started. They saw club promoters putting their street team to work, passing out flyers and promoting the hottest parties for the weekend. Since they were already at the mall they decided to get outfits to wear for the game and one for the party tonight. So they head over to the hotel and checked into their rooms and got dressed for the tonight's game.

Through Davante's inside connections he was able to get two good floor seats for the game that evening. His seat was in a great position so that every time his future client scores he will give him this look like, let's get this money. Davante would give him this nod basically saying keep doing your thing. He was sure the 15 thousands fans in attendance and the millions watching on television had no clue of their relationship. Davante just knew as long as his client stayed focused and keep his stats up he is considered a Lottery pick and would be at least picked in the top 3 of this years NBA draft. His parents wanted him to come back for his sophomore year, but due to his draft status this year, he can't take a chance on getting injured next season or his stock would drop instantly. So far Davante has him set up with a 1 million dollar insurance policy for this season, just to protect him. So after the game, they went back to their hotel rooms to get so fresh and so clean. Davante made a call to some friends that lived in the Atlanta area, because he knew they would know where all of the hottest upscale parties would be. That way they didn't have to worry about fights breaking out and random shooting going on in the younger adults night clubs. They went to this nice upscale club that was located not far from Buckhead. There were a lot of single beautiful women ready to mingle inside this place. Davante and a few of his friends were just chilling and having a good time near the bar, enjoying the scenery and out of the blue a young lady walks by and said I have noticed you since you walked in. Here's my business card, but if you except my business card you must meet me over there by the restroom so we can have a better conversation while you are not with your boys and I'm not with my girls. Their eyes got locked in for a quick moment. Davante told her I except. He notice her from the beginning as he saw her walking through the crowd earlier, it was something about her walk that was so seductive, he knew a lot had to do with her standing eye to eye with me. He knew for some men that height on a women may be a turnoff, some guys are intimidated, but for him that would be a turn on. Along with her beauty and a pretty smile, she will get him every time. Not only was she tall with a sexy walk but she had like her own style and swag. Davante told his boys give me a minute I'll be right back.

As he approach her he could smell her perfume. And there is nothing better than a women that's sexy and smells good. First thing he said to her was I have to admit your perfume smells good. She was like wow, well thank you, I guess I owe it to Clinique Happy the original.

He told her my name was Davante I'm a sports agent and Im here for business/pleasure and that he live in Florida. She was like what does pleasure mean in details? He laugh then he explain that going to a sporting event to see potential clients is considered pleasure.

She introduce herself as Yolanda from Detroit. She said I work in corporate America, I travel a lot due to my profession. As they continue talking more and more they both felt the chemistry between each other as the night continued, they danced and joked around with each other so much, they forgot that they both came with friends. As the club was closing neither of them wanted to leave each other side. She asked him where can we go this time of night that's still open to grab something to eat. Davante said I'm not sure, why don't you just call me once you are in your car and I will navigate myself to the nearest restaurant. She call him and ask why don't we just meet up first and we can just drive behind you. Since he had already drove off he had to pull over on the highway and gave her direction to where he was currently at.

Since they both were from out of town they couldn't think of a any place that would be serving food this time of morning. Then after driving they realized they had two options of getting something to eat and suggested Denny's or Waffle house. Davante was sure they were open because they are 24 hours in any state. He then approach a Denny's and notice a Waffle House directly across the street. While on the phone she said ok sweetie tell me which restaurant you want to eat at.

He told her since me and one of my home boys came down here together, he will be joining us. She was like that's cool because I'm with my homegirl as well. It was crazy because they had no idea where they were at. It was 2 in the morning and the city was still packed due to all the people in town for the final four. She finally caught up with them and then they located the restaurant. While they sat, not sure if Davante friend and her friend ever connected but I know they both never lost sight of each other. After they ate their breakfast they both was like I really don't won't this moment to end. But they both knew out of respect for their friends they had to depart. They kept in contact and they both said whoever travels first they must make an effort to see each other. A couple of months went by and she told Davante she was going to be in Beaufort, SC on a business trip and would love to see him. He told her since that's only a two hour drive for him, you best believe he will be there. As he approach her hotel room all he could hear is some old school R&B by Babyface. He knocked on the door and when the door open he was thrown back by how gorgeous this women was. Just her whole attitude was so up lifting and she made him feel like she took her time and planned her whole day making this moment perfect for them. She said I hope you are hungry because I have a surprise for you.

He told her actually he's starving. She said great, because I made a candlelight dinner of one my favorite Spanish dish that I personally made for you and some sweet red wine. Then after they ate dinner, she said I have a special dessert that I think you are going to love. After hearing how Yolanda has planned their evening made him become a lil closer in feelings towards this woman. As he began to take his jacket off so he could get comfortable, she was like no babe let me help you with that. She was like today is all about you, because I'm sure I will have my day also(hint). As they sat at the table, they both held each other hands as he blessed the food. They sat there ate and had great conversation talking about family, work, life and love.

He ask her where do you see yourself in 3 years? Her answer

was hopefully married to you. It caught him off guard, but he didn't knock the idea. Yolanda said all jokes a side because of my heritage in my family we are known to be married. I'm sure you see Spanish family sticking with there man and most Spanish women are not going anywhere. So just to let you know.

You have a ride or die chick right here.

As they finished up with dinner she said let me gather these plates and I will be right back with desert. As he sat and waited he loosen his belt because she definitely filled his stomach.

She said I will be there in a second. He leaned back in the chair with a sigh of relief. She walks up behind him, kind of startle him. And she puts a chocolate covered strawberry in his mouth gently. As he's chewing she begins to start kissing on his ears. She then places another chocolate covered strawberry in his mouth and started rubbing her tongue on the back of his neck. At this point he's breathing a lil harder. He reached behind him and started rubbing on her legs. Then she turns the chair around so that he could face her. As he's facing Yolanda he notice she is wearing a all white button down shirt. She begins to place her legs over his legs and straddle him. She then place a strawberry in her mouth and lean towards him so they both can share the same strawberries. As they both bite gently into the strawberries their lips touch. They began kissing slowly. She then start grinding on him as he caresses her.

Then he slowly start to unbutton her shirt. One button at a time as they continue to kiss softly. Once he got to the last button he noticed Yolanda was completely naked and all he saw was a beautiful peach tone color skin. He then lifted her warm heated body up as she wraps her legs around his waistline. He carried her to the bedroom as they kiss. He laid her down gently on the bed.

He then placed her legs on top of his shoulders as he start kissing on her inner thighs.

As he got closer between her legs he felt the tension of her expectation of wanting to be fulfilled.

He told her babe relax because your night, is now. He started licking his tongue over and around her Venus as he could hear her moan and groan. He kept kissing her Venus as it becomes moist and then he begin to slide his tongue inside slowly. Licking back and fourth on the Venus.

She was like babe I'm not like every women. He said what do you mean. She said when I cum I cum.

It's going to be a lot babe I just want to warn you. He said babe when I said it's your night I meant that, so if that includes tasting all of you. Give me every drop. Now relax as I take care of you. As he hold both of her feet with his hands he can feel her toes curling.

He continue licking, kissing and nibbling between her thighs as she screams while her ecstasy begins pouring out like a waterfall. He quickly took off his pants so that he could plug her waterfall from this overflow of juices. As he begin to put it inside she begins talking to him in Spanish. He didn't understand her, but it sounded sexy as hell. Then she translated in English by saying popi hurry and give me that big Mars. He noticed she likes talking shit while having sex. She kept asking for it. For a moment it didn't feel like they were making love nor having sex.

It felt like they were fighting in a one round battle and they were trying to see who was going to get knock out first. They tore that bed up. They knocked the mattress on the floor.

She were digging her nails in his back, but with the sex being so good it took his mind of the pain.

After they were done it seemed to be a draw. They both agreed to take a quick break and go at it again. They agreed but only on one condition, he get to tie her hands together so she can stop those paws from killing him. She agreed and they went on to a second round, starting in the same place they stop at. He believe they tried at least 15 different positions. They rolled over again, she got on top and started riding him from the back like as if she was riding a wild bull. He must had the best view in the world, because he was able to physically see how Yolanda was working every muscle in her back and hip. Then she started playing in her long silky black hair as she continued riding him, which he thought that was so sexy. He must admit he was dealing with a professional and he had to bring his A game to the bedroom.

Every time she came down he lift up giving her every inch of his Mars as she yells out his name. He knew after this round it wouldn't be another stroke in his body. She told him babe I'm ready to tap out, he told her he have been tapped out, he just wanted to make sure that he pleased her first then drained her for all your juices. She was like babe you took everything out of me and then some. I don't think I can feel my legs. Didn't you feel how my legs were throbbing?

He said he thought it was a small earthquake that had the room shaking. Ok, she said I see you got jokes. She said I'm only 35 but I'm feeling like I'm 65. She said can we just lay down on this floor while you hold me. He said sure thing babe. He offered to get her something to drink out of the kitchen. She said no babe, I just want to lay next to you. He hold her in his arms while she laid on his chest.

He knew at that moment thinking about how she made this evening special for them that she wants to be the only women in his life. They both talked about family, friends and future and within 10 minutes they both were sound asleep.

Chapter 3

Caucasian

DAVANTE GOT A phone call this morning from a radio station in Des Moines, Iowa. They wanted to talk with me about an endorsement deal for one of his clients. After finding out which client they were talking about they explained that they wanted his NFL starting Linebacker from the Pittsburgh Steelers. They wanted him to come out and do some public appearances in the city, and to judge a cheerleading contest for their newly franchise Arena Football team.

Davante said fax over the contract so he can talk with his client and get back to them within 30 minutes. Once his client committed to the terms, Davante faxed over the contract. The Radio Station executive called after receiving the fax to explain that once Davante and his client arrived in town, they will have someone from the radio station waiting to pick them up at the airport.

So Davante contacted Ms Roberson his travel agent and told her he needed two 1st class tickets for Des Moines, Iowa and he will not be needing a rental car for this trip, but at least two hotel rooms for them. Ms Roberson said give me about two hours and I will call you or text you your flight confirmation. This will be for Saturday and Sunday and come back on Monday?

Yes ma'am, your the best. When Davante and client arrived, the city welcomed them with open arms. Shelby the marketing director for the local radio station was there to pick them up from the airport. She was very nice, very helpful and very beautiful. She ask how was the flight? Well Besides someones new born that was crying the entire flight, it was okay. Shelby said, I'm so sorry to here that. Well I'm here to assist you guys with anything you need. I want to make sure your stay here in Iowa is memorable. Maybe you will come back and visit.

So let's first go over to the radio station. Let me ask are you guys hungry? Davante quickly said yes as a matter of fact we are. What is it that Iowa is known for because that's what we want. Shelby replied that we are known for having the best tenderloin Steaks. Ok that's what I'm talking about. Well as a matter of fact there is a nice spot that's in our direction as we head towards the station. When were finish we need to get to the station because we need to let the listeners know that your client is in town. We also need to let them know, that he will be one of the judges at the Mall today, to select the cheerleaders for the cities newest Arena Football team. We will have him ask the fans to come out and show their support. But I'm sure with your client being in town and with Iowa having a huge Steelers fan base we won't have any problem having a big crowd. Davante replied, that sounds like a good plan to me. Once they got to the station they got the opportunity to meet everyone. His client then got on the air and begin promoting the events for today and answering questions from callers. As time goes by, Davante and his client did a few hours hanging out at the radio station. Mean while Davante and Shelby were having a conversation, getting to know each other and everything else about the city and things to do outdoors and how the event should go. Davante realized that him and Shelby had a few things in common. They both were big fans of Kung fu movies and PBR(Professional Bull Riding). As they talk and laugh Davante's client thought they were odd balls.

As they finished up at the radio station, Shelby drove around the city giving them a little site seeing. She drove them by the arena where the Iowa Barnstormers will be playing their first home game of the season. She took them to a beautiful neighborhood where most of the homes are listed in the millions. She ask Davante's client if you decide to move here in Des Moines, Iowa this is definitely the area you would want to live because it has everything at your disposal. Davante then ask Shelby to take them to the neighborhoods you don't see on television. He explained that he's not always interested in seeing places where the wealthy live. He likes to see how other people live as well.

He likes seeing any neighborhood wherever he goes that include the areas where people really don't care for seeing like urban neighborhoods. He stated I guess I'm different. He claims he do it because, it always reminds him where he's from, and It is motivation to keep pushing him towards bigger and better things in life. As they approach a red light a gentleman started cleaning the windshield and asking, can he clean the windshield for a dollar. Davante said it didn't look like they had a choice, because he had already started cleaning it, before he could answer. Davante rolled down his window and gave the guy a fifty dollar bill and told him he can keep the change. The expression on his face was priceless. He acted as if God had answered his prayers. He said thank you, thank you, God bless you. Then he turned to Shelby and said this is why he love seeing all people. Shelby was really impressed. She said ok I see how you like doing things. You believe in taking care of people in need. She looked away real slow. Davante's client looked at him and was like Davante did you just see what I saw? He was like I sure did. So as they continued driving through the neighborhoods, time was approaching for the judging of the cheerleaders at the mall. So they started heading in that direction. As they approach the mall they noticed the parking lot was packed. As they made their way through the mall, they were escorted to the center area by two security officers. Right from the beginning they noticed 25 beautiful ladies. All they kept saying was how are they going to narrow this down to the best 12 cheerleader's. After all the rules were explained and given to them, they realized that the ladies will eventually eliminate themselves from their performance. Shelby ask Davante if it was ok for her to sit next to him? Davante told her that he would love for her to sit next to him.

As time goes by, they are now down to the final 12 females. The announcer mentioned that there will be an after party tonight with the 12 newest cheerleaders along with Davante's NFL client in VIP. All he was thinking was ok, I'm starting to love what the city has to offer. He asked Shelby was she going to be their chauffeur for tonight? She said no actually, there will be a limo picking you guys up from your hotel room. But she advised them that she will definitely be at the party. Well, since we're finish here, we need to be going so I can get you both back to your hotel rooms so you can get all cleaned up. Shelby look at Davante just before he got out of the car and said I'm looking forward to seeing you tonight. He told her so am I. As time passed, the front desk call him and said hello Mr. Davante your ride is waiting downstairs. He called his client to see if he was ready and to tell him to meet him downstairs. There was a gentlemen standing in front of a stretched all white Cadillac Escalade. Good evening gentleman my name is Xavier, I will be your chauffeur for this evening. Davante's client looked at him and said they really know how to make a brother feel special out here in Iowa. As they approach the club they noticed how long that line was for people waiting to get in. He texted Shelby to see if she was already inside, she text back saying give me like two minutes and I'm pulling up. They sat and waited, there were people trying to peak through the tinted window to see who's inside. Shelby tapped on the glass Davante rolled down the window and she was like come on lets go. Davante and his client stepped out, Davante grabbed Shelby's hand as they walk past the crowd, people were yelling out his clients name, waving and showing him love. They got to the door, two bouncers escorted them to the VIP section. For the first time since they got out the limo Davante had a chance to really look at Shelby. He told her before it gets crazy in here he wanted her to know that they came in here together and he's expecting him and her to leave here together. He told her that she is really wearing that black dress and that she smells amazing. He asked by the way what is that your wearing? She told him Versace Yellow diamond. He asked her so he don't have to worry about some jealous boyfriend running up on him in here tonight since he's an outsider? She said Davante that is the least of your worries.

He leaned over and kissed her on the cheek. Now this place is starting to get packed and the DJ was on point. He kept giving shouts out to his NFL client in VIP while everyone's trying to get a picture of him, but the security has already informed them that they will not let anyone in VIP for pictures or autographs unless its approved by them first. The waiter kept bringing champagne for everyone in VIP. There were a lot of gorgeous women in VIP, but his mind was already made up that none of them were looking sexier than Shelby. He told his client to make sure you enjoy yourself tonight, but always make sure you make smart decision and nothing stupid that will hurt your image. Shelby walked up to them and said I hate to bother you

Davante, but can you please come with me. Davante was like where do you have to go?

She said I need to go to the ladies room, but I really don't feel like fighting thru that crowd by myself. He was like ok cool I'll take you. She said thank you so much. He said sweetie you don't have to thank me. He said come on let's go, I'll lead. As they walked through the crowd, He noticed a girl staring at him as they were about to pass. She brushed up against him and said, so no sister's were good enough? He acted as if he didn't hear her and kept walking through the crowd while holding Shelby's hand. They finally made it to the other side of the club. He said go ahead, while you're in there let me run into the men's room. We will meet right back here. Shelby said Davante why did you chose to be with me tonight. It looks like you wouldn't have any problems finding a beautiful women in here. I watched you, you definitely get a lot of attention. I'm sure that's wherever you go. You have this aroma about you when you walk into a room full of people. Some people have it and some people don't. You have it, I noticed that girl trying to flirt with you and she knew we were together.

Let me explain Shelby like I said before, we came in here together we are leaving together. Everything I'm doing with you, is everything I wanted too. I'm attracted to you so you have nothing to worry about. I got you. He leaned over and whispered in her ear and said I want you. Come on let's head back. They finally made it back to VIP. Ok, let me mingle for a lil bit and I will be right back. He made some great connections for some other events for him client to attend.

Everyone was having a great time. He decided to go and sit next to Shelby since she seemed like she was not having a good time and she would rather be any place else besides here.

He jokingly told her he noticed her from across the room and he just had to come over here and introduce himself. He told her she must be single because no man in his right mind will let her come out alone looking as good as she did. She replied well actually I'm not alone, the man I want, I'm leaving with him once I leave here. He said oh really, do I know this guy? She replied, you might know of him. He's tall, Caramel complexion, well built, clean cut, handsome and sexy as hell. Damn sounds like you got yourself an amazing man. Hold on to him tight because he sounds like a keeper. She replied, that's what I'm planning on doing starting tonight. Now you do realize that we don't have to stay until this place close. She replied you don't have to tell me twice. He told her to give me a second let me tell my client we are about to leave. He told his client he's about to take off, but his client was so occupied by two ladies, he just looked at him and gave him the nod and was like ok handle your business and we'll get up tomorrow before our flight. He was like cool. He grabbed Shelby by the hand as they walked thru the crowd.

He told the limo driver Xavier to take them to his room and come back here and wait for his client because he is still inside. He told Shelby to leave her car in the parking lot of the club and they will figure out a way to get it tomorrow. Xavier closed the door behind them as they both got into the escalade. Shelby looked at him and started smiling, then she slid of her shoes and used her left foot and started sliding it up and down his leg. He told her don't start something you can't finish. She was like, I always finish what I start. Then she started sliding her foot between his legs. Now she's starting to get him aroused. He felt him beginning to wake up.

She had this sexual look in her eyes that if he could read her mind, it clearly says, I'm going to do some things to you tonight boy that will certainly have your toes curling. She then started pointing at him asking him to come closer. As he began to lean forward, she grabbed his hand and placed his hands behind her neck. She then starts rubbing her hands up and down on his thighs getting a feel of the bulge in his pants while bitting down on her bottom lip and smiling. He started rubbing on her shoulders softly while sliding his hands down one side of her dress until his hands reach her waistline. He could feel the threads of her panty line, wrapped around her small frame waist. She placed her hand on his chest and pushed him back and started slowly zipping down his pants. He noticed her nipples started getting really perky as they showed through the dress, he then started caressing her nipples with each of his finger tips causing her to moan seductively. She then proceeds to cores his Mars by rubbing her hand from the top to the bottom very slowly as if she was trying to do her on measurement, then while taking it completely out of his pants. She then begin to slowly kiss around the head a few times while making it soaking wet with the juices in her mouth. She then begins to place the entire head into her mouth and gently squeeze down with her tongue. At this time he began to help her finish undressing himself by taking his pants and underwear completely off. Now as she has his head completely wet, she then proceed to loosen the one strap that was completely holding her dress together. As she kneel in front of him, he slowly pulled down her sexy black lace underwear. He used his right hand to pull it over her ankles and his left hand to pull her closer to him by placing his hand behind her head as she go up and down on his Mars. She then began to get off her knees, turned around with her back facing towards him and threw her legs over his thighs as she then began to straddle him. She then reached behind her to get a good grip on his Mars and rubbed it around the tip of her Venus to get her body adjusted for what it was about to take on. She began to slowly slide down on it inch by inch until all was completely covered. She moans out oh my God, it's to big, but she continues to slide up and down.

She placed both hands on his knees and rode him like a pro. As she became completely wet, he then turned her completely around while it was still inside her, as she sat facing him, she grabs him by the back of his head and started grinding slowly and proceed to go up and down fast, like as if they were running out of time. He then gently leaned over and started kissing her breast slowly. Then he started licking her nipples getting them wet and blowing his cool breath on them. He could feel her nails digging deeper into his skin as she continues to grind on him, but because of the pleasure she was giving him, he couldn't worry about the pain. She then leaned back, place both her hands on each of his legs and continued to grind on him as she kept calling his name out loud. He asked her does this Mars feel good, she replied words cannot explain how good you are giving me this Mars. She then said babe, I want it from the back I love that position, so he lifted her up till she reached the top of his manhood, he slowly turned her around once again, while she used her arms to help hold her body weight as she slowly slides down his Mars from the back. She started going up and down as he held on to her waist.

She said babe move your hands I got this and she proceeded grinding on him in circles.

As he wrapped her hair around his hand she kept asking for him to pull it harder. He knew she was climaxing because he felted her thighs becoming soaking wet as she kept taking it in and out. She then begin sliding completely all the way down slowly taking her time enjoying every inch. Then she started going up and down fast as he spanked her and continued pulling her hair.

He then slid his hand between her thighs and rubbed the front of her Venus as she moved in circles. She's begging him not to stop. They kept going for about 20 minutes in that same position. She yelled I can't hold it babe, I'm coming again, baby I'm coming. Her body shivered, he could feel her releasing multiple orgasms. Her legs began throbbing afterwards. She said oh my gosh, that had to be the best I ever had. You almost made me say I love you. He told her you just did and smile. The limo driver announced we will be at our destination in few minutes.

He told Shelby, he wanted to go another round. But this time his job is to get you to say the words I almost got you to say earlier. That's going to be my challenge to you. She said challenge accepted.

Chapter 4

DAVANTE IS BACK in town for a few days, he's exhausted with seeing clients and meeting parents. He said the next two days is going to be nothing but relaxation for him. He called up Tim and James his other two best friends that's not married. He's like what's going on fellas? Tim, what up big homie, you in Town? Yes, I flew in late last night. I will be home for about three days. About to get up and surprise my kids by picking them up from school. I'm free this evening.

I'm thinking about hitting our spot around 6pm. Ok cool that will work. I will see you guys there later. James was like that's cool because I will be already on that side of town so I will just meet you guys up there. Davante's alarm went off about 1:30pm which was set for him to get up and head out to his two kids school. As he get to his daughter school first because she gets out at 2:30pm. As she was standing outside waiting on her mom she saw me pulled up and was ecstatic and joyful. He ask her for some reason you look like you was happy to see me.

She was like daddy. Seriously. I'm always happy to see you. Now where have you been?

My baby girl always have questions for her dad. Lol. I was out of town taking care of business. You always out of town. Well baby girl that's part of my job. But you do know I'm just a phone call away and he told her you and your brother that can call me anytime you want.

As we approach his son school he saw him talking with his friends. Davante blew his horn several times before he noticed him. Then he started running towards us. His daughter said and you better be running to that back seat. His son ask dad why she always in the front seat.

His daughter said because she is the oldest. He said you two stop it. I'm happy to see you both and I miss you guys. Hey I'm taking you guys to Disney world this weekend. But right now let's get some ice cream before I drop you both off.

It's now about 4:30pm which gives him enough time to go home and shower.

It's now about 5:30 pm as he driving to the spot his daughter Riley called to see what I was doing. Hey daddy what are you doing. Hey baby girl, nothing much going over here to meet up with James and Tim. Oh ok. Are you ok? Yes I was just watching tv and was thinking about you. That's my girl, I love you, I love you to daddy. Where is that big head boy? In the room doing homework. You wanna talk with him. No if he's doing school work let him do that and just tell him to call me when he's done. Ok. Daddy can you pick us up from school again tomorrow.

Yes baby girl I will. Make sure you let your mom know. Ok. Alright I will talk with you later.

Davante arrives at the bar James was already sitting down. What's up man, dang you better leave those weights along. Man I'm trying to get you and Tim in that weight room. I told you Greg and John got a membership there about 6 months ago. Oh ok cool. How them two fools doing?

They good still living that marriage life. Man they can have that, man I'm trying to get that.

Man you tripping. Tim walks in fellas, what's up. Who tripping, what I miss? James, man Davante over here talking about he wanna be married. Tim, you okay homie? You not getting soft on us are you? No man, real talk I really been looking to find my soulmate. But not just that, I'm looking to date outside race and if I find true love, then my soulmate is going to be whatever nationally she is. Tim, now we talked about this the other day, so how are you going to settle down and find her, if all the women keep throwing themselves at you? I know it's hard homie, because you don't know who to trust. And you just like me. You not really attracted to the women who comes after you, you more attracted to the women you find, who gives you a challenge, but not too much of a challenge. James, man just date one of those Brazilian girls, they fine.

Yeah I know, but I always remember those words my aunt told me, everything that looks good on the outside doesn't mean it looks good in the inside.

Tim, man you sure you not talking like this because your ex-wife married that white boy last year? No it's not that, its bigger than that. Funny you said that because she always jokes with me saying if you want peace in your life you better jump ship. I told her that's what got me in trouble with her, jumping ship. James, yells waiter, please bring us some drinks and bring three shots because my boy Davante over here talking about love and marriage. It's giving me the heebie-jeebies. Tim, man you know you our boy so whatever you want we gonna support you, just make sure I'm the best man. But on the real, we just trying to make sure if that's what you really want. For me love should have no color and right now my happiness is more important than the completion of someones skin tone. Can

I truly bond, will her family except me, how would making love to a women of a different race actually feel, will there be chemistry, would we listen to the same music in the car, can we relate when racial issues comes up, will we agree or disagree together? I feel I need to know than not know. I feel if I don't at least try, I will never know who my future true wife could be if I don't start now. I ask the question is every woman the same, or is every women different? If so, what makes women different, besides the color of their skin and the texture of their hair? What separates these women apart? It's important knowing your worth and having someone appreciate everything about you, the good as well as the bad. We can be waiting until we get old to find that women from the same race that may or may not show up or we can just except a good women no matter what color. Tim, you know every women is the same. The same how, Tim man I don't know, I just hear they are. Well that's it, for me I need to know. I need to feel, I need to experience, I need to see how we bond and I need to see if chemistry is there. I can't and I will never answer these questions if I don't at least give it a try. James, well right now I need you two to give these damn shots a try. Man you in town let's get off the subject about being in love with this race or that race and tell me who you think is going to win the Super Bowl.

Is your client from the New York Jets still having that party on Saturday? I know you, when that party start you will cut your ringer off. Man you know you two are my boys, but I have to cut my phone off, because everyone be calling me either to get them in free or trying to get VIP passes. Just because I have the connections doesn't mean I can help everyone get in. Now you see why I cut my phone off. I feel you man.

Davante tells his friends jokingly that he will be married next year. They don't believe him because they feel he's living a bachelor life and they tell him constantly why mess up a good thing. He didn't want to settle, he didn't want a woman that wanted him, he wanted to find her. He is a Leo and wanted the challenge of being the hunter.

Chapter 5

African American

IT'S FRIDAY 2PM east coast time and he got a call. Hello. Hi may I speak to Davante please.

You are speaking with him. Great this Ed Sullivan, the general manager of the Chicago Bears, how are you? I'm great and I would even be better if you are calling to tell me we have a long term contract in place for my client. Well actually that's the purpose of my call. Well that is great news to hear. Well with a contract of this magnitude, I would prefer flying in first thing Monday morning and talk face to face so we can get this contract signed. I know my client has been waiting patiently for this deal to go through. Well Mr. Sullivan I appreciate the call and I will be looking forward to seeing you next week Monday lets say 2pm Central time. Sounds great, will see you then. Davante called his client and told him the great news. I'm flying out there Monday morning and we will not settle for that Franchize tag they were trying to give you. I will continue to argue for what you are worth especially after last year breakout season. You are the number one linebacker in the NFL. With those stats you are worth a 5 year $70million dollars with $25millions dollars guaranteed. I will keep you posted and hit you up once I'm there because I will e-Fax you the contract, sign it and send it right back.

Alright cool, sounds good to me. Davante hung up with him and call his travel agent. Ms Roberson how are you today? I'm great. Where are you flying to now and what time you must be there?

Well I don't have to be there till Monday but see what you can find for me this evening to Chicago and I will fly back on Tuesday morning. Not a problem I got you, will you need a rental and hotel? No just the hotel please. Your the best. I hear you. You just make sure I get those Jaguar tickets so I can take my son. I know how your friends get, once the season starts they want those NBA and NFL tickets. Before I forget thank you for that Autograph picture of Lebron James, my son is so excited. He's adding it to all his collectibles. I think You need to start selling those tickets.

I bet that will slow them down from asking for free tickets. Ok, You know I got you Ms Roberson. Since he's heading out to Chicago Davante called his friend Angel since she's from chi town. At least he will have someone to show him the city and besides, he has known Angel for about a year and she is defiantly marriage material considering he's ready to settle down and find the women of his dreams. Davante never forgot how he and Angel met. Last year he was in Indianapolis, for the NFL combine. At the hotel where he was staying which had a gift shop downstairs. He was looking for two souvenir gifts to purchase for his son and daughter.

He got his son a Indianapolis Colts watch and as he was getting a Pink Colts T shirt for his daughter he noticed a beautiful lady with a name tag on. He said excuse me do you have this shirt in a medium? She replied I'm not sure, why don't you ask someone that works here?

He said I am, I notice the name tag. She was like oh my god I can't believe I'm still wearing my name tag. I'm sorry but I don't work here and besides aren't you to big for a medium pink shirt and smile.

He explain no it's for his daughter in Florida. Whenever I traveled I always try to get them something. Them? How many kids do you have? Two, I have a son name lil Davante and a daughter name Riley, let me show you a picture of them. They are beautiful. Wow a proud father. Yes I am. Those two right there is my world.

Your wife must be a lucky woman. No me and their mom have been divorce for over two years now. I'm sorry. Don't be because my ex wife and I have a great relationship for the sake of the kids. By the way I'm Davante and you are "Angel" yes indeed. Excuse me!!!! Nothing, so you mentioned Florida is that where you currently live or you live here in Indianapolis? I just like shopping at hotel gift shops. Lol. Ok I see we have a comedian. Is that your full time or part time job? No I'm just kidding, I'm full of life and laughter is good. But no actually I'm a flight attendant, I got an overlay here. So I'm stuck here til tomorrow. But I'm from Chicago.

The Windy City. Have you ever been there? Yes a few times, I'm not big on cold weather.

I know I will be there next year. Ok cool, are you going to the hotel gift shop there as well? Funny, actually I was coming to see you. Oh really. Now I see you are a comedian as well.

Her phone rings, she said excuse me give me a second. Hello this is Angel. Oh no. Well ok I understand, thank you. Is everything ok? Yes that was my job now they are saying I can't leave until the day after tomorrow. Wow. I'm sorry to hear that. Well look at the bright side you have met a friend who will also be here for the next two days. If you like, why don't we find something fun to do this evening. Ok that sounds great. There is a ice skating ring next door. Ohhh I can't ice skate, actually I have never been. Well perfect. First time for everything.

Man I will be out their busting my behind. No I will be there to catch you. Yeah right. No I'm serious. Ok let's say we meet up downstairs in the lobby in about two hours. Is that good for you? Sure, well let me pay for my items. Are you getting that magazine you have been folding up for the past 30 minutes? Yes I am. Don't worry I'll get it for you. Oh thank you. That's so sweet of you. Ok then my treat at the Ice Skating rink. Ok Cool. Then I will see you in a couple of hours. Time went by he came down stairs in the lobby and Angel was already there, looking beautiful. He was like wow, your serious about seeing me fall. She just smile. They went to the ice skating rink. As they sat down and put on their skates, he ask Angel now if I fall you have to promise me that will be our secret. Angel said don't worry what happens in Indianapolis, stays in Indianapolis.

Angel said give me your hands, I got you. Angel had to hold one of his hands while he hold onto the railing with the other hand. They were having such a great time. They were getting a little upset because for the first time he found something that he could not do. They laughed all night because he kept falling. He was like ok my butt is sore from falling. Let's take a break, she was like oh pour baby has sore buttock. Need a massage?

Heyyyyyy don't touch my buttcheecks. She laughed, ok let me just try to make it over here to these chairs. As they sit down they talk and they were just was being themselves. Davante really enjoyed that moment he had, getting the opportunity to know more about Angel, what she wanted as far as her career and relationship goals. He ask her what do you have planned tomorrow evening? Angel said probably sitting up in my room. Well, If you like NBA basketball the Chicago Bulls will be playing. Maybe we can catch the game on the big screen at the bar downstairs. That sounds great, actually I'm a huge bulls fan. I actually played college ball. Really??? Yes really, oh cause you see a woman wearing heels, you don't think she has game. No, I didn't say that I just couldn't picture you playing. What that means? I met you in your business attire so that's all I know. When or if I see you in something different I will judge you by that. Hmmmmm. Ok.

Cool. So let's say about 7:30pm, no let's make it closer to 8pm. I'm a woman you know we take just a tiny bit longer. Oh I'm sorry I thought only women in Florida takes longer so I guess that's everywhere. Ok comedian, alright let's get up out of hear. Ok I enjoyed every moment with you tonight. And I'm looking forward to tomorrow. I'm feeling the same way. I really enjoyed my time with you Mr. Davante. He gave her a hug. I will see you later. In the morning he had phone calls after phone calls. Davante spoke with his client and told him tomorrow he needs him to focus when he is at combine. Play it how you played the game in college. You will impress every NFL scout. Get some rest and I will see you tomorrow. As time was approaching for his date with Angel. As He was getting dress he call his kids on speaker phone and told them he has a surprise for them. They both kept asking what it is it dad. Tell me, tell me. Did you buy us a puppy? No it's not a puppy. You guys are not ready for a dog. Yes we are, he can clean with us and play with us. Yeah ok, well I would have to talk with your mom about that one. Oooooookkkkkkk, stop sounding so sad. Well you guys be good, I love you and I will be picking you both up from school on Wednesday. Ok. Love you Daddy. Now it's 7:45pm, he decided to get there before she does so he can already have a seat available. Now its about 7:58pm.

He's wondering if she is a woman of her word and shows up on time. He's looking and he didn't see her coming, but he noticed a woman walking towards him in a red dress as she comes closer, he realize that it was Angel. His heart drop, this woman had to be the most gorgeous woman he has seen in a long time. She said you didn't think I was coming? No I believe you were coming, I was just thinking, she probably going to make it closer to half time. But I must admit, I'm impressed, with the time and I am ultimately impressed with the way you look wearing that dress. I see you got your hair down, simply beautiful. Ahh thank you. You also smell amazing. What's that you are wearing? It's Prada Candy. I wanted to wear something red to support my Bulls. Let me get this chair for you. They watch the game and converse getting to know each other better.

They didn't want the night to end. So she Invited him upstairs to her hotel room.

They laid across the bed and pillow talk. They talked until they both dozed off. The next morning they woke up with him holding her from behind. They both agreed that with him holding her felt so good. She had to fly back to Chicago that morning and he had one more day in Indianapolis. They always remain friends and kept in touch. Throughout that year they always talked about meeting up but they both never seem to make time. So when he told Angel he will be in Chicago for a few days, they both were looking forward to it. She knew a lot about him even all down to my favorite color. When he landed in Chicago, she insisted he don't get a rental since he's in her home town wherever he need to go she'll take him. So he agreed.

When he got of the plane Angel was standing there with this red fitted tank top shirt and some black jeans, that showed every curve she was blessed with. She look like she just came straight from an Ebony magazine photo shoot. Angel definitely had brains and beauty. They instantly connected like they did a year ago when they met. He gave her the biggest and warmest hug possible as she leans in to kiss him. It caught them both of guard. They both talked about it but never acted on it until now. Then he looked into her eyes and slowly lean into kiss her back.

He said wow, I'm finally here in the Windy City with Ms Angel. She said by about time.

I was starting to think you were afraid of cold weather. Well you do know that Florida weather will definitely spoil you? Actually I don't know, since I haven't gotten my invitation. Hint, ok I got you. Hey babe is it ok for you to take me to run some errands? Babe you don't have to ask, that's why I'm here.

Angel took him to a few of his appointments. One of his clients called and ask if they can talk in private when they meet up. He said that's no problem. Angel over heard them talking and said babe please drop me off home and take care of your business. I will just be waiting at the house for you. She was like you have the GPS in the car so you should be ok. After meeting with his client and talking business he started heading back to Angels place. He called to find out if there's anything she needed while he was out. She replied just you, I hope you didn't eat yet. because I have a surprise for you. He said actually he haven't. As he pulled into the garage he noticed she left the door slightly open. As he walked closer to the door, he noticed the place slightly dark. She comes to the door while wearing a sexy red lingerie. She puts her fingers over his mouth and says shhhhhh I got you. She takes his hand and walks him to the kitchen and said if it's ok with you I would like to feed you the the dinner I prepared for you. I made you a seafood dish with lobster and my famous dipping sauce. When he got to the kitchen he noticed she had made candlelight dinner. He thought it was so sexy of her for doing this for him.

After dinner she took his hand once again an pulls him to the back. Once they arrived to her bedroom he noticed candles all around the edges of the garden tub. The water was filled with pure white bubble bath and rose peddles. Angel then starts slowly undressing him. Then she begins to unbutton his shirt, while giving him small kisses on his chest. Then she slowly pulls down his zipper and takes off his pants, underwear, socks and shoes. He slowly got into the warm water Angel prepared, she told him to relax and let her handle this. She begins to bath him like he was her King, she fed him chocolate covered strawberries. She poured them both a glass of moscato wine. She had Sade song playing "The Sweetest Taboo". He must admit she is really making an impact on how he's feeling towards her. He's feeling so good at this moment he has goose bumps all over his body. Then Angel stood up in front of him while he laid back in the garden tub and begin to slowly start undressing her red lingerie in front of him. It was like watching the sunset over the ocean. Just an amazing scene.

She then slowly gets inside the garden tub with him. As he laid back she stood over him and starts to bend down, but he stopped her and said stand here for a moment, as he began to kiss her thighs and slowly started kissing around her Venus, he began sliding his tongue inside her Venus. She flinched, then she grabs his head and hold gently with a tight squeeze. She starts breathing heavily and the more he heard her moan the more he continued to please her. She then placed both hands on the wall and begins calling out his name, she then place one hand on his forehead and said baby please don't stop. He continue to taste her and with every gentle thrust she exhale breathlessly. She ask baby I need to feel you. Right now, as he continued to lick all the edges around her Venus, she could hardly get a complete sentence out. He held her by her waist and he slowly guided her to where she wanted to go. He was so turned on, his Mars was completely hard as a rock. She grab it and hold it in place, so she could land directly on it. She said oh my God I can feel every vein you have babe, its so thick and long, please don't hurt me. He said babe I will only give you what you can take. As she goes up and down nice and slow. She grabs him by the back of his head and start shaking and said no I don't wanna cum this fast but I can't control it. He ask her to let it go and that we have all night.

I will give it to you anyway you ever dream of having it. They made out on the bathroom counter next. Then he picked her up and then carried her to the bedroom while still laying his Mars inside of her Venus. She ask baby, let me turn around and I want you to give it to me real good from the back. I know you like being in control so baby here is your chance. Get it how you want it baby. The more wet her juices begin to flow the more inches she was able to receive. She then said ok babe lay down, I got this. It's my turn to take control. Im going to ride the hell out of your Mars until I can't ride no more. He took a deep breathe and before you know it Angel was just riding me. Placing her hands on his chest going up and down like a pro, he could feel all her juices coming out and dripping all over his body. She said ok babe let me lay on my side and I want you to give it to me fast with some long deep strokes. He was loving how Angel wanted to take charge of every position.

Davante automatically knew his Job was not done until he knew Angel was 100% sexually satisfied. Angel then started screaming and said baby, I can't hold it I'm about to cum all over you. He said babe let it go. Give me every drip your body has to offer. I wanna make sure your body never forgets me. She said babe as of now your name is written all over this body.

So you can start contacting UHAL and we will figure out who's going to be moving me or you.

Chapter 6

Asian

DAVANTE HAD A friend name Lin he met online a while back, they kept in contact for years.

There was nothing big between them, but they always wondered what it would be like to finally meet each other in person. She lives in Los Angeles, California and because there are no NFL team his time in that city would be limited. Even thou they do have the Los Angeles Lakers and Clippers, he just don't have any NBA clients playing for neither team. Whenever he flew to Oakland, California which was just hours away from Lin, she was normally out of town herself.

One day it so happens that they both were going to be in Denver, Colorado. He told Lin that he will be in Denver in August during the NFL preseason to make sure his client signs his rookie contract with the Denver, Broncos before the regular season starts. He is the only 1st round draft pick that haven't sign as of yet, because we have been waiting to see if they were going to resign Payton Manning to a long term contract. Since they gave him a Franchise tag for one season last year, he need to get his client a long term contract because he is planning on being the face of that franchise like John Elway did for so many years. Davante should be flying out of Florida on

Friday morning and arriving in Denver around 12noon. He has a 2pm meeting with the general manager and Vice President of football operation. He's hoping to have this contract signed over the weekend. So by the time Lin arrives in Denver on Sunday he will have plenty of time for them to spend quality time together. He will have them two box seats in the owners suite to watch the game on Sunday. Ok, that sounds awesome. I can not wait to see you. I'm super excited. I'm excited as well. I will text you once I landed to at least let you know I made it there safely. I will be waiting to hear from you on Sunday to make sure that you made it in safely as well. Ok babe I will do. Once Davante landed, he sent Lin a text so that she knew he made it in town safely. He went on and conducted all of his business meetings that he had planned for my trip that day. He was excited because everything the team was talking about when it came to his client was positive. They were getting the deal they asked for after an intense contract negotiations. As Sunday approaches, Davante get a text Sunday morning saying hey babe just wanted you to know I made it in town safe, just picking up the rental and I will be seeing you later. Smiley face, he texted Lin back later telling her he's leaving his Hotel room now heading to the stadium and that's where he will be waiting for her.

She said text me once your out there so I can tell you where I'm at doing that moment.

Lin texted me and said she was about 10 minutes away. He texted her back and said awesome, I will be downstairs in front of Will Call with the tickets waiting for you.

He wasn't sure what to expect from a California girl being around all these wild Denver Broncos fans. Since they never met in person he wanted to throw her off by telling her to look for a guy wearing a red suit with red shoes and that he was 5'5 about 250 lbs. She kept saying stop playing with me, because I promise if I see a round guy in a red suit I'm leaving. Davante said ok I'm sorry, I have on a blue suit. She said Davante don't play with me. I'm kidding, relax I just wanted to make you laugh. As he continues to wait he saw thousands of fans everywhere getting ready for this game against the Seattle Seahawks. As he looked into the crowd, he noticed first, someone walking towards his direction with a sexy walk and sexy legs to go along. That walk she had as she continues to get closer to him made everything seems to be moving in slow motion. She was wearing a yellow fitted dress that made the sun look like it didn't exist anymore. She was toned and had an aurora about her as she approaches. As he's reaching to hug her she kisses him on the side of his face. They both said finally at the same time and started laughing. He told her I'm glad you excepted my invitation, she said or you serious this is a chance of a life time. I get to meet the infamous Mr. Davante. Plus I get to attend a game with him. For the record I'm a settle Seahawks fan, he just smiled. He grab her hands as they walked thru security. As they started going up the escalator towards the suite she would not stop staring. He ask her what's wrong, she said red Suit and 5'5 huh, he said I was just trying to keep you on your toes. She said it's been over a year and besides I've seen enough photos of you and heard your voice so I knew better, but it was cute though. As they locate their suite he noticed Payton Manning in the hallway, as he approached us, he shock my hands and said congratulations on the contract your client is going to be a very special player for this franchise. He said thank you and can you please take him under your wings and teach him to be great like yourself? He said I got you, Lin ask him do you think I can take a picture with Payton?

He said I don't think he would mind, but out of respect let me ask him. He ask if my lady friend can take a picture with you? He was like sure, we all family now!!! Lin was like that's amazing in your line of work you get to meet all the great athletes. Davante was like it's just like any other profession, it has it's ups and downs. As they continue to walk down the hall Lin suddenly squeeze his hands tighter. He said babe are you ok? She said Im OK, but did you notice those 3 Asian men staring at us? He said yes, I noticed but I'm not concerned your with me.

Lin said I know babe, but as we walk passed they spoke in Chinese. What did they say?

They said "I guess he couldn't find a women of his race". Wow that's funny, Now if you like we can go back and I can say actually I did find someone of my race, and kiss you in front of them. No babe, now we can go back and you can just kiss me in front of them. That's funny, let's not let simple minded people ruin our time. So as they made it to their suite, they first noticed how loaded this room was with a Buffet of all you can eat hors d'oeuvres and drinks. They were other fans inside the suite so they introduce themselves and made their way to their seats and enjoyed the view. Since Davante's client signed the contract on Friday, the coach told Davante he was going to let him start the first quarter, just so he can get a feel of how fast pace the NFL game is. As they sat there Lin was really into the game and to his surprise, she was very knowledgeable about the plays and calls, he was very impressed. She kept asking him every time his drink got low or his plate was half empty would you like anything babe? He was like no I'm good, but thank you. As they watched the first quarter, he was very happy of his clients performance. They saw the second quarter and Davante told Lin "let's take off I've seen enough", he's not going to play again today, and besides everyone else who plays, are the ones who's looking to make that 55 man roster final cut. Besides if we leave now we can beat the crowd. I caught the cab here, I didn't need a rental because I knew I was doing everything around the stadium on this trip. Lin said I rented a car so babe come ride with me.

After they located her car, he asked is there anything you would like do are maybe catch a movie or something? She was like boy you made me wait a year to see you, so I'm sorry, I don't want to see a movie, the only thing I want to see babe is you. He was like cool, then let's head over to my hotel since its two blocks away. As they approached the rental car, he went and opened her car door and kissed her before she got in. As he came around, he noticed Lin reached over and opened his side of the door. He just smiled and took a mental note.

As Lin was driving he couldn't help but to notice her thighs and seeing how toned her legs were. She must have read his mind, because she gently grabbed his hand and placed it on the same thigh he was looking at. They finally arrived at the hotel. The concierge opened their doors and took Lin's keys. Once they got into the room, Davante told Lin to make herself comfortable while he open the blinds, you could see that the sun was just about to settle behind the mountains. Lin was like that's a beautiful sight, he said yes it is. She said no I'm talking about how good you look standing at that window with that beautiful view of the sunset behind you. He said it would be even better if it was behind us not just me. Davante reached out for her hands as he pulled Lin closer, he whispered in her ear, that it really means a lot to him that you made time for us to be together today, and because of that I'm going to make sure your trip to Denver will never be unforgettable. As he squeezed Lin gently with his arms around her body as her head laid against his chest, he kissed her softly on her forehead and said let's take a shower together, I believe I have a shirt you can wear. If you are tired we can lay on the bed and pillow talk or I can give you a full body massage to help relax you. She was like babe you don't have to ask me twice. The chemistry we had, It felt like we have been together for years. Davante took her by the hand as they both walked towards the bathroom. They both started taking off their clothes in front of each other while staring in each other's eyes. Not only was he impressed by her personality and smile, but Lin had a beautiful bronze complexion. As they began to get in the shower, so he could start getting the water warm enough for them, Lin said oh wait give me a second. She went to get her cell phone and brought it back with her to the bathroom, he's standing under the shower head as the water pours down his face, all of a sudden he heard "You are so special" by Kem. He said that's my jam, I love that song. She said I know, I remembered every song you said you love, so I made a playlist with all of them. Baby when I said I was into you, I really meant it and I saved all my love just for this moment. Lin walks up behind him and begins to give him gentle kisses on his back, she then place her hands on his chest from behind and started rubbing his chest and caressing his nipples while making them extremely hard. He could feel her warm naked body as she pressed up against his. She starts rubbing his shoulders while she continued kissing on his back and telling him "baby you have no idea, I dreamed of this moment". He told her I knew, because this was how you said you wanted to make love to me first, which was in the shower.

So as you can see, I also remember everything you told me as well. She said I'm impressed.

She then reached for the body wash and then she started washing him off from head to toe.

He extended his arms out as she continues to wash his entire body. She said babe turned around. As he turned she begin washing and rubbing him down. Then he began to reach for a sponge and pour body wash all over her and the sponge. As he washed off her body, Davante massaged her body as well. Their eyes connected, he begin to kiss her slowly, he then rubbed his hands slowly off her shoulders down to her waste, he placed both hands around her waist and slowly lift her in the air while she places her legs over his shoulder. She gently placed both hands on top of his head while squeezing harder as he began kissing the insides of her thighs. He then began to kiss the front of her Venus and follow up with kisses around it. Then he began licking it nice and slow. He didn't stop until he could feel her juices flowing. Then he started tasting her over and over again. She then kept saying yes, yes, yes, Davante, every time he sucked gently on her Venus. He then lifted her off his shoulders and slide her down his body nice and slow. It is such a sexy view watching the water drip off your beautiful face and body. He began wiping the water off her face as he slowly kiss her beautiful face. He then slowly turn Lin around and ask her to hold on to her ankles while he please her with the pleasure of love. He started slapping her gently with his Mars in a playful way on her butt, he then begin to tease her a little by putting just the head of the Mars in and taking it out. Lin said babe stop playing and give it to me, baby please give it to me. He then began to rub the Mars around her Venus as the water drips of her body. He then slide the head of his Mars in as he felt her flinch. He slowly started sliding more inches inside her Venus until she can no longer take more.

Then he began stroking it nice and slow while he grabbed a hold off both bottom, slowly giving her every inch just how she wanted it. He started grinding her and switching up a little by going in deep with long circular motion. She said damn babe you killing me with all that. As he started grinding upwards he notice every time he would push, he was lifting Lin to her toes while in the shower. He kept pushing every inch of his Mars in and slowly pulling it out to the tip of the head over and over again. Watching her in the shower while making love to her had my body in such of an intense feeling. He couldn't hold it back any longer. He told her baby I'm getting ready to let it go. she said wait babe, I want to taste your love. He said babe it's coming, do you want it all, she said yes I want every drip love. Davante was trying to find anything to hold on to as he grab the faucet and shower head feeling like he was pulling it out of the walls. She grabbed his Mars with both hands like she was holding a baseball bat, she took all of his energy from him and continue holding his Mars until he was completely drained. He told her babe lets finish up washing off because I'm not not sure how much longer my legs will let me stand. They both finished up washing off, he wrapped Lin in a towel and dried off her entire body. He then rubbed body lotion over her body from head to toe. Then placed my big t-shirt on Lin, kiss her and said give me a second and I will be in the room. Davante got himself together came in the room completely naked and laid in the bed with Lin under the covers. They pillow talked about everything for about 30 minutes, until she fell asleep on his chest. As they laid there all he kept thinking about was how beautiful Lin is on the outside and inside. She was special and made him feel a certain way.

He didn't know if what he and Lin had was love or lust, he just knew that it was a feeling he never wanted to let go off. She felt good, taste good and everything else any man would want and need, Lin had it.

Chapter 7

AFTER HIS EXPERIENCE with these four beautiful ladies from different ethnic backgrounds, he came to realize that it doesn't matter when it comes to race, nationality or lifestyle. However, woman are different in their own ways as far as personality, attitudes, cooking style, perfume, clothing, music and religious belief. It's really about what you expect from your significant other and how her presence makes you both feel emotionally that makes the difference. Ask yourself the question is there a true connection between you two, can you have a bond with this person that can't be broken, can you see this person not only as a best friend but as well as your soulmate. A great conversation to have would be getting to know what that women likes and doesn't like. Understanding what you both will tolerate and not tolerate. We must remember that once we become adults many of us are already set in our own ways. So in order to find true love we should not change drastically for someone, however we should make adjustments. Let's put our egos to the side and watch how far your love will blossom. It's no secret that women have emotional needs. But once a man has reassured that women that all her needs are met, he will become a satisfied man, because most women love to please their man. Being physical is easy especially if you both are mutually attracted to each other, but having that women satisfy your needs because she appreciates you and wants to show you that she wants you in her life, you got yourself a winner. Keep in mind every women wants to feel special, secured, protected and loved by her significant other. Every women also would like to be treated like a queen and to have a man that not only she knows, but feels in her heart that she is the only women in his life. If you give a women the attention she needs, she would become the happiest and loyal women in the world.

Chapter 8

DAVANTE DECIDED TO have a Christmas party to celebrate a great year of contracts negotiations. Since he wanted to invite his family and friends to celebrate with him, he contacted his travel agent to ask her if she knows of someone who can create an e flyer invitation for a Christmas party he was having. She said wait I can do that for you. But first I need to know am I getting an invitation first. Yes, you know you are my girl, I got you, awesome. Well send me an email or text including all the information that you want on the invitation. Now, if you have everyone's email or their cell numbers, I can get the invitations out to each one of them. Wow, you can do all that. Hey Davante, I have brains and beauty ok. I'm not mad at you. Well I'm still paying you for your time ok. That's fine just add it to the next time you book a flight somewhere. I'm glad you said that because I need you to book a flight for this party. Why are you flying out if your having a party? No I'm having someone fly in for the party. So I want you to take care of the flight, hotel and limousine service. Wow, who do you have coming the President? Your funny, I will get back to you on all the details for that later and everyone else's contact information. Davante got on his phone to contact his tailor. Hey what's good man? Nothing much just working smarter not harder, I hear you, Hey I'm having a Christmas party in 3 weeks I need you to come by and get me fitted for a black Armani suit and I wanna get a pair of those Gucci shoes you showed me the last time I was there.

Ok you the man, you know I got you. I got and opening next week Monday at 2pm. Awesome. I will see you then. Davante then contacted his sister and told her about the Christmas party and that she would be receiving and invitation shortly with all the details. He was more so excited for her to meet the women that he's planning on settling down with. Considering the last woman she knew he was serious with was his ex wife two years ago. She said wow about time. I'm happy for you, I prayed for this moment that you find someone that's going to make you happy. So what's her name and where is she from? Wow, so many questions. Just know that I'm happy and I feel she is the one for me. It was a long time coming. But I feel everything happens for a reason. I have met some amazing women in my two year journey of being a bachelor, but at some point in my life I have to follow my heart. My heart has led me back to her. It's a feeling I can't explain, but I know it's a feeling I don't want to lose. Ok Sis let me run some errands. I will see you at the party, love you. It's finally the night of the Christmas party and his travel agent called him to tell him that the Limousine driver just got a call that your guest is ready for pick up from her hotel room. That's awesome do you know if the dress that was left for her in the room needed to be altered. I think it will fit perfectly because I had the seamstress contact her for adjustments and she said it fits perfectly. Wow, Davante you know your women size down to a tee. Don't worry, I didn't forget, not only was the dress in her room you picked out, but I got the flowers of her colors you wanted and her favorite candy. Ms. Roberson you're the best. No, it just seems this women here is special and that she really means a lot to you. So I just wanted to make sure everything goes the way you had it planned. Thank you so much.

Chapter 9

AS THE NIGHT finally arrived Davante walked downstairs wearing a Black Armani suit with a pair of Gucci shoes wearing his favorite cologne "Bond No. 9 Chez Bond" to open the door for the guest he has been excited to see. As he opens the door he's greeted with a smile that can lighten any dark room.

Davante said you look so beautiful and you are definitely wearing that dress.

I guess I owe it all to you. It is my pleasure. Now Davante, you know I'm still in shock. I kept asking myself why me?

"Davante you are a smart, tall, Carmel complexion, chiseled body, very humble, great personality and a successful 35 year old black man in America. You get plenty of attention from women. "Why me"? Well, why not you? All those women you mentioned did have my attention, but none of them had my heart and the chemistry like we do. Sex doesn't keep a man.

That's what separate you from everyone else. You are my Queen. I fell in love with you spiritually and emotionally before I even thought of you physically.

You're everything and more that I need in my life and I would be a fool to let all that go away. When a man knows he has found that one woman he have been searching for, he changes everything for her.

Sometimes we search for true love in all the wrong places and most of the time if we would just open our eyes we would find her. My eyes and heart is wide open for you and I'm not planning on closing it until I take my last breath knowing I gave all my love to you.

Ever since we had our first conversation it was all platonic. I honestly had no idea we would be at this point months later. It went from seeing you at times, then looking for you, then wanting to be with you. Finding true love has no destination but I'm sure predetermined of where you belong is destined.

We instantly connected with just a friendly conversation.

I started realizing that not only we had a lot of things in common, but it was so easy for us both to open up and talk with each other about any and everything. The more we talk the more I felt I found a true friend in you, and it's a feeling I never want to loose.

Why did it seem like I was being put on the spot when I came through that door? It seem like everyone had just seen a ghost and It seemed that I was the ghost. (with a laugh)

No sweetie, I'm sorry you felt that way, it's just that I have been dating and not once have I ever introduce any one to my friends, family and especially my kids until now.

WOW, I'm flattered. I invited you because all of the times we have talked you caught my attention with every word you spoke. I consider you my best friend and I'm just gonna put this out there I would love the opportunity for us to take our friendship to the next level. It's no secret that I'm attracted to you. I'm at ease with our conversations and many of times we talk all night on the phone and half of the times it wasn't about anything. That's just to show you, being on the phone with you is all I need. It doesn't matter how much money we both happen to make, if we can't share it with the person we love, it's pointless.

You are a beautiful, smart, intelligent professional woman and I love hearing the passion in your voice when you talk about your family, career and your marketing firm. I love the fact that you love sports. So it's definitely easy to just chill with you and not hang out at the sports bar with guys all day.

I love the fact that you believe in eating healthy, staying in shape working out and considering we both love working out. I would be crazy to keep going on looking at you as the girl from the gym. I want more from you, I want more for us. A women like you comes around every century, and I'm 35 now and I don't want to wait another century, but I would love the opportunity for us to be as one until the next century comes around. Now I can go on for hours telling you how much you mean to me. But let's face it, you are definitely beautiful, but that's not what attracted me to you. I feel for your personality and our conversations. I am willing to take things slow, because I don't won't to lose what we have accomplished thus far, because there is a time and place for everything and this time right here, is a time I will never forget.

And that's to be in love with my best friend.

Davante you gonna make me cry, I promise I'm not trying, I'm just being real and speaking from my heart. I know sweetie, please hold me. Davante promise me you will be good to me, promise me that you will love me only, promise me you will never let me go, promise me you will protect me. "Lori" I promise, I got you. We are one, ok before we go over here to introduce you to my kids and my family. You might wanna go clear up your eyes. Ohh I'm so sorry. No it's cool, we had a deep conversation so it's cool if it gets emotional. Come on I'll walk with you over to the ladies room. Davante held his arms out and said right this way Ms. Lori. She says says mmmmmmm you smell good. Well thank you

After you Mr. Davante. Giggles

Printed in the United States
by Baker & Taylor Publisher Services